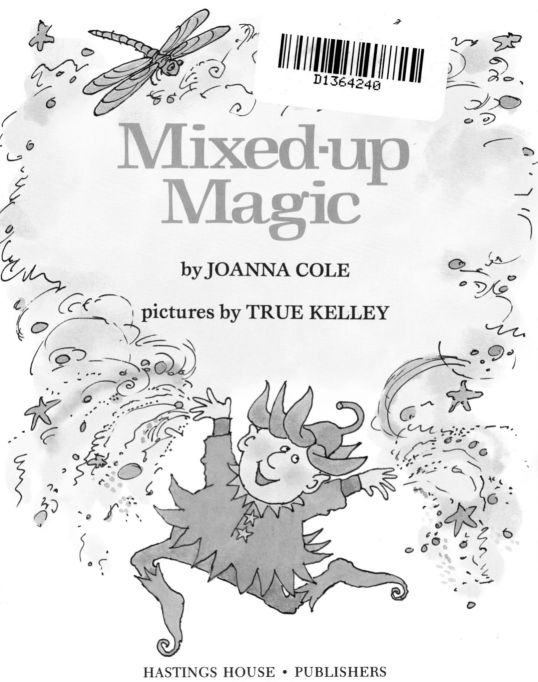

Mixed-up Magic

by JOANNA COLE

pictures by TRUE KELLEY

HASTINGS HOUSE • PUBLISHERS
New York

This edition is published in 1987 by Hastings House by arrangement with Scholastic, Inc.
Text copyright © 1987 by Joanna Cole.
Illustrations copyright © 1987 by True Kelley.

For information regarding permission, write to Scholastic Inc., 730 Broadway, New York, NY 10003.

Library of Congress Cataloging-in-Publication Data
Cole, Joanna.
 Mixed-up magic.

 Summary: Maggie meets a kindly, boastful elf who never quite fulfills the wish he means to grant.
 [1. Wishes—Fiction. 2. Elves—Fiction.
3. Magic—Fiction] I. Kelley, True, ill. II. Title.
PZ7.C67346Mi 1987   [E]   87-14965
ISBN 0-8038-9298-5
Hastings House, Publishers
9 E. 40th Street
New York, New York 10016

Art direction/design by Diana Hrisinko.

Distributed to the trade by: Kampmann & Company, Inc. New York, New York

Printed in the U.S.A.

10 9 8 7 6 5 4 3 2 1

7155775

To Tracy and Kristen Olson
—J.C.

To Jamaica T. Kelley
—T.K.

Maggie lived all by herself
in a little house.
She had a little garden,
and that was about all .
she had.

One day, Maggie
was out in her garden.
She pushed back a leaf—
and there stood
a funny little man.

"Who are you?" Maggie asked.

"I am an elf," the little man said.
"And I am magic."

"Can you make a wish come true?"
  Maggie asked.

"That's what I do best,"
  said the elf.
"I am the best wish-giver
  in the whole, wide world."

  Maggie looked at her old, torn coat.
"Well, then, I wish I had
  a new coat," she said.

"You shall have one,"
  said the elf.

He closed his eyes and said,
**"Oat, toat,
  Here's a coat!"**

But instead of a coat...

there was a goat.
"Maa-aa," it said.

"I wished for a coat,"
said Maggie.
"Not a goat."

The elf turned red.
"You will have a coat,"
he said,
"in a minute."

Maggie waited.
The elf tried again.
**"Oat, toat,
Here's a coat!"**

Then, suddenly,
there was a boat
in the middle
of her garden.

"Silly elf,"
she said.
"I don't need a boat."

"No problem," said the elf.
"Remember,
I am the *best*.
This time you will have a coat."

But Maggie did not get the coat.
Instead…

she got a moat
all around her house.

"Elf!" cried Maggie.
"Please be careful!
  I did not want a moat.
  I did not want a boat.
  I did not want a goat.
  I wanted a coat,
  and I still do!"

"Coats are too hard,"
  said the elf.
"Wish for something else."

Maggie looked at her old, worn hat.
"Okay, I wish for a new hat,"
she said.

"You shall have it,"
said the elf.
**"Tat, spat,
Here's a hat."**

All at once,
there was a cat
in the middle
of Maggie's garden.

"Oh, elf.
I cannot wear a cat
on my head!"
said Maggie.

The elf tried again and again.
Maggie got a bat...

a mat...

and a rat.

But no hat.

"Little elf,"
    said Maggie.
"Please stop.
    Your magic is all mixed up!"

"Let me try again,"
  begged the elf.
"Please, please,
  wish for something else."

"I will wish one more time,"
  said Maggie.
  She wiggled her toes
  through the holes in her socks.
"I wish for some new socks."

"Lox, mox,
  Here are socks!"
  said the elf.

All at once,
there was a fox.

"NO!" shouted Maggie.
"I want socks!"

"Wait," begged the elf.
"I know I can do it!"
**"Lox, mox,
Here are socks!"**
He said it four times, fast.

Maggie got a box,
two docks,
and a pile of rocks.

"Stop! Stop! Stop!"
 cried Maggie.
"Look at my garden!"

The elf began to cry.
"I guess am *not*
the best wish-giver
after all."

"Don't cry, elf,"
said Maggie.
"You did your best.
But what are we going to do
with all these things?"

The elf helped Maggie.
Together they tied the boat
to one of the docks.

They built a bridge
with the pile of rocks.

They tied up the goat
and let it eat grass.

They told the cat
to chase away
the rat and the bat.

They put down the mat
so the cat could sleep.

And they put the fox
in the box
and mailed it
to the zoo.

When they were all done,
Maggie and the elf
went for a ride
in the boat.

"I am sorry, Maggie,"
said the elf.
"I did not make any of your wishes
come true.
I will try again."

"No! Please don't!"
cried Maggie.

"But you did not
get anything you wanted,"
said the elf.

"I did not get anything
I *wished* for,"
said Maggie.
"But I think
I got something I *wanted*."

"What is that?"
asked the elf.

"I always wanted a friend,"
said Maggie.
"And I think you are my friend."

"Yes, I am,"
said the elf.
"I am the best friend
in the whole, wide world."

It was true.
Maggie and the elf were friends
from then on.
And Maggie even got the new
coat, hat, and socks she wanted.

When she wished for a float...

she got a coat.
When she wished for a pat...

she got a hat.

And when she wished for an ox…

Maggie got a terrific pair
of new yellow socks.